Favorite Stories from Cowgirl Kate and Cocoa
Rain or Shine

Written By
Erica Silverman

Painted By
Betsy Lewin

🦅 sandpiper
Green Light Readers
Houghton Mifflin Harcourt
Boston   New York

To Tricia Gardella, Hali Mundy, Lynne Olson,
Sylvia Patton, Karyl Thorn, and Judy Weedman,
my trusted advisors on all things horse —E.S.

To Chopper, who doesn't like the rain —B.L.

Text copyright © 2008 by Erica Silverman
Illustrations copyright © 2008 by Betsy Lewin

First Green Light Readers edition, 2013

www.hmhbooks.com

The text type was set in Filosofia Regular.
The illustrations in this book were done in watercolors
on Strathmore one-ply Bristol paper.

The Library of Congress cataloged the hardcover edition of
Cowgirl Kate and Cocoa: Rain or Shine as follows:
Silverman, Erica.
Cowgirl Kate and Cocoa: rain or shine/Erica Silverman: [illustrated by] Betsy Lewin.
p. cm.
Summary: Cowgirl Kate and her cowhorse, Cocoa, discover what it means to work, play, and be
together—rain or shine.
ISBN: 978-0-15-205384-0 hardcover
ISBN: 978-0-15-206602-4 paperback
[1. Cowgirls—Fiction. 2. Horses—Fiction. 3. Rain and rainfall—Fiction.]
I. Lewin, Betsy. Ill. II. Title. III. Title: Rain or Shine.
PZ7.S58625Cok 2008
[E]—dc22
2006032363

ISBN: 978-0-544-10503-4 paper over board
ISBN: 978-0-544-10502-7 paperback

Manufactured in China
SCP 10 9 8 7 6 5 4 3 2 1

4500421856

Prancing in the Rain

"I'm tired of staying inside," said Cocoa.

"I want to go out and play."

"It's still raining," said Cowgirl Kate.

"Let me put on your rain sheet."

"No!" cried Cocoa.

"I look silly in my rain sheet!"

"Jumper is wearing *his* rain sheet,"
said Cowgirl Kate.

"He looks silly," said Cocoa.

"But he'll stay dry," said Cowgirl Kate.

"I'd rather get wet!" said Cocoa.

And he trotted outside.

Rain fell on Cocoa. He shook it off.

He kicked up his hooves.

He pranced into the corral.

He pranced past Jumper.

He pranced—

SPLAT! SPLASH!—

into a puddle.

Rain fell harder.

It soaked Cocoa's coat.

It drenched his mane.

Cold raindrops rolled down his neck.

Cocoa shivered.

He looked at Jumper.

Jumper was not dripping wet.

He was not shivering.

Jumper does not look silly at all,
thought Cocoa. *He looks dry.*

Cocoa trotted back into the barn.

"You look like a wet mop," said Cowgirl Kate.

"I feel like a wet mop," said Cocoa.

Cowgirl Kate rubbed him down.

She wrung the water out of his tail.

She brushed the mud out of his mane.

"That's better," she said.

"Yes," said Cocoa.

"And *now* I will wear my rain sheet."

Cowgirl Kate put on his rain sheet.

"Cocoa," she said,

"you look good in your rain sheet."

She held up a mirror.

Cocoa whinnied.

"Yes," he agreed.

"And I look *much* better than Jumper."

11

Chasing the Rainbow

Cocoa peeked into Cowgirl Kate's window.

"Wake up!" he said.

"The rain has stopped."

Cowgirl Kate opened her eyes.

"Yeehaw!" she shouted.

Cowgirl Kate got dressed.

Then she crawled through the window

and climbed onto Cocoa's back.

"Giddyup!" she called.

Cocoa trotted to the south pasture.

"Moo, moo," mooed the cows.

"Moo, moo, moo."

"The cows sure are moo-ing," said Cocoa.

"The cows always moo," said Cowgirl Kate.

"Yes," said Cocoa,

"but they moo even more after the rain."

Cowgirl Kate sniffed the air.

"The air sure smells fresh," she said.

"You always say the air smells fresh,"
said Cocoa.

"Yes," said Cowgirl Kate,

"but it smells even fresher after the rain."

Cocoa nibbled some grass.

"The grass sure tastes sweet," he said.

"You always say the grass tastes sweet,"
 said Cowgirl Kate.

"Yes," said Cocoa,

"but it tastes even sweeter after the rain."

"Look, Cocoa," cried Cowgirl Kate,

"there's a rainbow!"

"Lets's go!" squealed Cocoa.

"Let's find the pot of oats at the end of
the rainbow!"

And off he went at a brisk trot.

"Cocoa," said Cowgirl Kate,

"we will never reach the end of the rainbow."

"Yes, we will!" cried Cocoa.

On and on he trotted.

On and on and *on* he trotted.

Finally, he stopped.

"The rainbow keeps moving away," he said.

"Rainbows are like that," said Cowgirl Kate.

Cocoa's head drooped.

"Then I will never find the pot of oats
at the end of the rainbow," he said.

"Maybe not," said Cowgirl Kate.

"But I know where we can find another one."

She rode Cocoa back to the barn.

She prepared warm oats.

She added molasses.

Cocoa snorted.

"That is not a *pot* of oats," he said.

"That is a *bucket* of oats."

But he gobbled them all up.

"Yum!" he said.

"Warm oats and molasses tastes
even better after the rain."
Cowgirl Kate smiled.
"I guess everything is better
after the rain," she said.
"Not everything," said Cocoa.
He nudged her gently.
"You and I," he said,
"rain or shine . . ."

"we are always just right."